Special thanks to Linda Chapman

To Maya Gardam,
who would be a perfect friend
for the Secret Kingdom

ORCHARD BOOKS
338 Euston Road, London NW1 3BH
Orchard Books Australia
Level 17/207 Kent Street, Sydney, NSW 2000
A Paperback Original

First published in 2013 by Orchard Books

Text © Hothouse Fiction Limited 2013

Illustrations © Orchard Books 2013

A CIP catalogue record for this book is available
from the British Library.

ISBN 978 1 40832 377 9

3 5 7 9 10 8 6 4

Printed in Great Britain by Clays Ltd, St Ives plc

The paper and board used in this paperback are natural recyclable
products made from wood grown in sustainable forests. The
manufacturing processes conform to the environmental regulations
of the country of origin.

Orchard Books is a division of Hachette Children's Books,
an Hachette UK company

www.hachette.co.uk

Series created by Hothouse Fiction

www.hothousefiction.com

Reading consultant: Prue Goodwin,
lecturer in literacy and children's books

Sugarsweet Bakery

ROSIE BANKS

ORCHARD

The Secret Kingdom

Sugarsweet Bakery

Contents

A Birthday Treat

It was a beautiful summer's day. The
blue sky was dotted with fluffy clouds
and the sun was shining down on
Honeyvale Park, which was filled with
people walking their dogs and feeding
the ducks. Over by the oak trees, Summer
Hammond's mum was setting out a
birthday picnic for one of Summer's little
brothers, Finn.

"Isn't it lovely today?" Summer asked her two best friends, Jasmine Smith and Ellie Macdonald.

Jasmine nodded, her dark ponytail bouncing up and down. "It's the perfect afternoon for a birthday picnic!"

"Let's go and see the ducks," Summer suggested.

"Wait," Ellie said. "Your mum's calling us." She pointed over to where Mrs Hammond was waving at them from a sea of colourful picnic blankets.

The girls ran over to see what she wanted.

"Girls, could you do me a favour please?" Mrs Hammond asked. "I need some help with one of the party games. Can you hide these stars before Finn and his friends arrive? Then, when they get here, they can all try to find them." She took a bag of silver cardboard stars from one of the picnic hampers.

"No problem, Mum," said Summer.

"Don't go too far away, and don't hide any too close to the duck pond – we don't want anyone falling in!" Mrs Hammond said with a smile.

The girls took the bag and set off around the park.

"Okay, let's split the stars up and each hide some," Jasmine said, handing handfuls of stars to Ellie and Summer.

The three girls ran off in separate

directions, hiding stars in bushes and in
hollowed-out tree trunks,
on benches and
near the edges
of flowerbeds.
Finally there was
just one star left.
Summer held it
up. "Where shall I
hide this?" she asked
as Ellie and Jasmine
walked back over to her.

"How about beside that bench by the
pond?" suggested Ellie. "It's not too close
to the water."

They all ran over. Jasmine moved some
of the long grass and bent down to hide
the star by the leg of the bench. But as
she did so, there was a loud croak and a

toad jumped out! Jasmine squealed and leaped back.

Ellie laughed. "Jasmine, it's only a toad!"

"I know, but it gave me a fright!" Jasmine giggled.

"Poor thing," Summer said, watching the little creature hop away. "I bet it was more scared of you, Jasmine!"

She watched the toad sadly as it
hopped away. It had reminded her
of their friend, King Merry. He was
the ruler of an amazing place called
the Secret Kingdom, which the girls
had discovered when they'd brought
a beautifully carved box home from
their school jumble sale. The box had
summoned them to the Secret Kingdom
so that they could help undo the trouble
that King Merry's awful sister, Queen
Malice, had caused when everyone in the
kingdom had decided that they wanted
King Merry to rule instead of her. With
the help of their pixie friend, Trixi, the
girls had managed to break Queen
Malice's spell and save the kingdom,
but now the queen had done something
even worse – she'd poisoned King Merry

with a terrible curse that was slowly transforming him into a stink toad!

"I do hope poor King Merry is okay," Summer said anxiously.

"Do you think he's starting to look like a toad?" Jasmine asked.

"Oh, I hope not," said Ellie. "If only we knew what the next ingredient in the counter-potion was!"

The girls knew that the only chance of curing King Merry was to make a special counter-potion from six rare ingredients. Jasmine, Summer and Ellie had already found the first ingredient, bubblebee honeycomb, but there were still five more ingredients left for them to get.

"Queen Malice is so mean," said Jasmine angrily. "I can't believe she's turning her own brother into a toad, all because she wants to rule the Secret Kingdom."

"I'd never do that to my brothers!" said Summer.

Jasmine pretended to look shocked. "Even after that time Finn put worms in your bed?"

"Well…" Summer grinned. "Maybe I'd turn him into a fluffy bunny, but not a stink toad!"

"Suuum-mer!" Mrs Hammond called. "Finn's here!"

Summer looked over to the stand of oak trees to see Finn arriving with his friends. She pushed thoughts of the Secret Kingdom to the back of her mind. "Come on!" she said to Ellie and Jasmine. "It looks like the party's about to start!"

Finn and his friends had a great time

at the party. They played pass the parcel and musical statues and then went on a hunt for the silver stars. "Don't go out of sight!" Mrs Hammond called as the boys raced away.

"Don't worry, Mum," Summer said. "We'll keep an eye on them!"

Jasmine, Summer and Ellie ran after the boys and made sure they didn't go too far. Within a few minutes, the boys had found almost all of the stars. Summer, Ellie and Jasmine gathered together, watching Finn and his friends hunting for the last couple of stars.

"Let's have a look at the Magic Box while everyone's busy," whispered Ellie. "Have you got it, Jasmine?"

"Of course!" Jasmine took the beautiful box out of the rucksack on her back.

Its sides were covered with carvings of mermaids, unicorns and other magical beings and there were six green jewels surrounding the mirror on its lid. Jasmine stroked the shining surface of the box and wished as hard as she could that it would call them back to the Secret Kingdom again.

"We've got all the stars, Summer!" Finn shouted, running over.

Jasmine hastily hid the box behind her back.

Finn skidded to a halt. "What's that?"

he asked. "Is it for me?"

"No." Summer laughed. "Not everything's a birthday present for you, Finn."

"But what *is* it?" Finn asked again. A few of his friends came running over and Finn pointed to Jasmine. "She's got something and she won't say what!"

"It's nothing," Jasmine insisted.

"There *is* something there!" Finn said,

trying to peek behind her back. "It's…
it's a torch or something. I can see light
shining from it!"

Ellie and Summer looked down at the
box. Sure enough, it was glowing!

"Hey, everyone!" Ellie exclaimed hastily. "I have an idea! Who wants to play hide and seek?"

"Me, me!" the boys yelled.

"Okay, guys," Ellie said. "You seek us first and then we'll look for you. Go and wait by the picnic rugs and count to a hundred."

The boys raced back towards the picnic site.

"Phew!" Jasmine sighed. "That was close!" She pulled the Magic Box out from behind her back. Its mirrored lid was still glowing brightly.

"The Secret Kingdom must need us!" said Summer excitedly. "Quick, let's get out of view so we can read the message." She pointed to a large patch of bushes nearby.

Jasmine, Ellie and Summer raced to the bushes and crawled underneath them. The bushes had high branches that formed a canopy overhead, and sitting under them was like being in a secret green cave.

Jasmine put the Magic Box down in front of her. Sparkling letters were already forming in the mirror.

"We're going to the Secret Kingdom again!" Summer said in delight.

"One thing's for sure," Ellie said with a grin. "Finn won't find us there!"

Off to the Secret Kingdom!

The glow from the Magic Box lit up the bushes as Jasmine read the message from Trixi:

"The next ingredient we seek
Is yummy, nice and oh so sweet!
Go to a place where all things bake,
Muffins, loaves and lots of cake!"

"Somewhere things *bake*," Ellie said thoughtfully.

"I wonder where that is," said Summer.

"And what the ingredient is," added Jasmine, her brown eyes shining.

Suddenly the Magic Box began to open. Inside, there were wooden compartments containing the six magical objects that the girls had gathered on their earlier adventures. As they watched, the magic map that King Merry had given them on their very first visit to the kingdom floated out of the box, unfolding itself before their eyes.

Jasmine plucked the map from the air and smoothed it out on the grass. It was like a window down onto the kingdom, and the girls could see the flags on the Enchanted Palace flying in the wind, the unicorns cantering around in Unicorn Valley and Clara Columbus, the imp explorer, striding along the steep sides of Bubble Volcano.

"Okay," Ellie said. "Let's see if we can work out where we need to go."

"Maybe the answer is King Merry's palace?" suggested Jasmine. "The elves bake all sorts of lovely food there."

Summer pushed her long blonde plaits back and scanned the map thoughtfully. Was there anywhere else that the clue might mean? Her eyes fell on a small building near Magic Mountain that she hadn't really noticed before. It was a friendly looking cottage, with a sloping roof covered with snow. A stream of pink smoke was blowing out from the chimney. Elves were hurrying in and out of the door, loading trays of fresh bread, cakes, pastries and biscuits into a carriage pulled by a beautiful white horse.

"What about this place?" Summer said excitedly. "It's called Sugarsweet Bakery!"

"Oh, yes!" exclaimed Ellie. "That sounds just right. A bakery would be full of yummy things!"

The girls covered the green gems on the lid of the Magic Box with their fingers and whispered, "The answer to the riddle is Sugarsweet Bakery!"

A bright purple light flashed through the air. They all blinked, and as they opened their eyes, they saw a little pixie floating in front of them on a leaf. Her messy blonde hair was poking out from under her flower hat and she was wearing a shiny green skirt and a matching top.

"Trixi!" Jasmine cried in delight.

"Hello, girls!" Trixi beamed. "Did you get my message?"

"Yes," Ellie said as Trixi landed on her shoulder. "How is King Merry doing? We're all so worried about him."

Trixi looked concerned. "He's croaking

more and more,"
she said. "But
that's why I'm
here." Her face
brightened.
"Aunt Maybelle
has discovered
the next
ingredient for the
counter-potion."

"Brilliant!" Jasmine
cried. "What is it?"

The girls looked at Trixi eagerly.

"It's silverspun sugar, the sweetest sugar
ever. Just a tiny bit of it will make any
cake or biscuit yummy and sweet."

"And it comes from Sugarsweet
Bakery?" Ellie said.

"Yes," said Trixi. "But it's not like

ordinary sugar. Silverspun sugar only appears once a year, at the end of the annual Sugarsweet Bakery cake-making competition. When the winner is announced, the silverspun sugar appears on the silver sugar tree that is planted in the bakery courtyard. The winner can use it in their baking all year long."

Jasmine frowned. "But if it only appears once a year, how are we going to get any?"

"It's the cake-making competition today!" Trixi announced excitedly. "Will you come to Sugarsweet Bakery with me and help find some silverspun sugar for the counter-potion?"

"Of course!" chorused Jasmine, Ellie and Summer.

Trixi pirouetted in delight. "Then hold

hands and get ready to go!"

As the girls joined hands, Trixi tapped her ring and chanted:

*"Good friends fly to break the curse,
Before King Merry gets much worse!"*

A cloud of sparkles shot out of her ring and whizzed round the girls in a glowing silver and lilac whirlwind.

Summer gripped Ellie and Jasmine's hands as she felt them all being lifted off the floor. Her heart pounded with excitement. She couldn't wait to see what Sugarsweet Bakery was like!

As the magic whirlwind whisked the girls away, they could hear the jingle of bells. When the sparkles cleared, the girls realised that they were sitting in a carriage being pulled by a white horse. The bells on the horse's reins were making a cheerful jingly sound, and there was a round, jolly-looking elf driving them along.

Ellie grinned at her friends, and her smile grew broader as she noticed that the beautiful tiaras they always wore when they were in the Secret Kingdom

had appeared on their heads. The tiaras
told everyone they met that they were
Very Important Friends of King Merry's.

"Next stop, Sugarsweet Bakery!" the
elf called as he pulled up in front of
the building they had seen on the map.
A delicious scent of fresh bread, cake
mixture, sugar and honey hung in the air.

"Mmm," Jasmine said.

"It smells amazing," agreed Ellie.

"And it looks good enough to eat!"
exclaimed Summer.

"It *is* good enough to eat!" Trixi
giggled. "Absolutely everything the
bakery is made from is edible."

"Wow!" breathed the girls. They all
stepped out of the carriage and walked
up to the bakery. Trixi was right – it
was a huge gingerbread house! It had

liquorice window frames with brightly coloured boiled-sweet glass. The window boxes were made of hollow candy-canes and sugar flowers stood inside them in marzipan pots.

Summer stepped forward to look at the white dusted roof. "It's not snow!" she said, running her finger along a window ledge and licking it. "It's icing sugar!"

"Come on," said Jasmine. "Let's go in."

Inside the bakery, there were counters everywhere laden with the most delicious-looking goodies Ellie, Summer and Jasmine had ever seen — cupcakes decorated with colourful swirls of buttercream, enormous sponge cakes with so many layers that they were almost as tall as the girls, huge round cheesecakes and chocolate cookies decorated with sugary glitter.

Jasmine's tummy gave a loud rumble.

Ellie felt her fingers itching for her colouring pencils. She loved drawing, and she

was longing to sketch all the amazing displays. She stared round, trying to remember every detail so that she could paint the scene later. Just as she was looking at a display of enormous round doughnuts drizzled with icing and oozing with jam, the door leading into the kitchens at the back of the bakery opened and an old elf came in. He was about as tall as Jasmine, but three times as round. He had pointed ears and his smiley face was plump and happy. He had an apron and a chef's hat on.

"Hello, can I—" he started saying, but broke off.

"Trixi! What a lovely surprise!"

"Hello, Albertin." Trixi smiled. "Albertin is the head baker here at Sugarsweet Bakery," she explained to the girls.

Albertin looked at the girls' tiaras and clapped his hands. A tiny cloud of flour puffed into the air as he did so. "Goodness me, you must be the human girls from the Other Realm! I've heard so much about you."

"This is Jasmine, Summer and Ellie," Trixi told him, pointing to each of the friends in turn. The girls smiled and shook hands with the elf.

"It's a pleasure to meet you!" Albertin said with a grin. "What brings you here today?"

"We're here because Queen Malice has been causing trouble again," Summer explained. "She's poisoned King Merry with a curse, and now…now…"

Albertin looked so worried that Summer couldn't continue. Even Trixi's blue eyes were filling with tears.

"Now, King Merry is turning into a stink toad," Ellie finished.

"We're going to stop Queen Malice, though," Jasmine told Albertin. "We're helping Trixi's Aunt Maybelle make a

counter-potion to cure him. We just need
to find all six ingredients required for the
potion."

"Poor King Merry!" Albertin exclaimed.
"I'm so pleased you girls are around to
fix things. But why are you *here*?"

"One of the ingredients for the
counter-potion is silverspun sugar,"
Jasmine explained. "Trixi told us that it
appears here once a year at the end of
your baking competition."

"It does," Albertin said proudly. "And
every single elf here adores the king,
so I am sure that whoever wins the
competition today will give you all the
silverspun sugar you need."

The girls looked at one another with
delight. Trixi blew her nose noisily and
smiled.

"Follow me," Albertin said as he headed off towards the kitchen.

Trixi grinned. "Elves are so lovely!"

"Wow," said Jasmine, breathing a sigh of relief. "This is going to be our easiest adventure yet!"

"All we have to do is watch the competition," Summer said happily.

"Ha!" A horrible voice cackled from behind them. "That's what you think!"

Trixi, Summer, Ellie and Jasmine all swung round and gasped in horror. There, standing in the doorway, was the tall bony figure of Queen Malice!

A Wicked Spell

"Queen Malice!" Trixi exclaimed.

The evil queen pointed her long black staff at the girls. "I'll never let you get the silverspun sugar!" she screeched.

Jasmine felt a rush of anger. "You can't stop us!" she said bravely. "The elves are lovely! Albertin said that whoever won would give us some."

"Oh, he did, did he?" Queen Malice snarled. "Well, we'll soon see about that!" She turned and pointed her staff at the kitchen door.

"From now, all kindly elves will turn
Mean and jealous, strict and stern.
They'll be horrid all day long,
Until the magic sugar's gone!"

She pounded her thunderbolt staff on the floor, and there was a loud crack and a flash of lightning. Suddenly sounds of crashing and smashing and voices shouting came from the kitchen.

"What's happening?" Ellie demanded.

"Enjoy your time here with the *lovely* elves!" Queen Malice cackled as she stormed out of the door.

Jasmine ran to the window and watched as Queen Malice took two black rats out of her pocket, put them down on the ground, raised her staff and fired a green flash of light at them. Suddenly a round carriage appeared, and the rats grew bigger and bigger until they were large enough to pull it. Queen Malice climbed inside, pounded her staff against the bottom of the carriage, and the rats raced away.

"It's okay," Jasmine told the others. "She's gone."

Before they could reply, the kitchen doors opened and Albertin strode back in. The friendly smile had completely vanished from his round face. "I thought I told you to follow me!" he snapped. "What are you doing still standing here?"

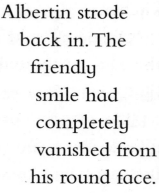

"Are you okay, Albertin?" Trixi said, zooming over to him on her leaf.

"Oh, go away, you annoying pixie!" Albertin snapped.

"It's the spell." Summer gasped. "It's made him horrible."

Just then, they heard another crash and some more yelling coming from the kitchen.

"Oh, dear," said Trixi. "It sounds like all the elves in the bakery have been affected by Queen Malice's awful spell!"

"Do you think the winning elf will still give us some silverspun sugar?" Jasmine asked Albertin anxiously.

"*Give* you some sugar?" Albertin glared at her angrily. "Of course none of the elves will just *give* you some, you rude child! If you want some silverspun sugar, then you'll have to enter the competition just like everyone else!" He huffed. "Pesky pixies and humans, wanting stuff for free. Hrumph!" With that he marched grumpily back into the kitchen.

The girls and Trixi looked at one another in dismay.

"What are we going to do now?" Summer asked.

Ellie ran a hand through her curly red hair. "I guess we'll just have to enter the competition and win the sugar for ourselves."

"Yeah," agreed Summer. "We can do it! Jasmine, you're really good at making cakes. You can lead the team."

Trixi shook her head sadly. "You don't understand!" she cried. "It's impossible for you girls to win. Each cake is judged not only by how it tastes, but by how spectacular it is. The elves don't just make their cakes delicious — they make them magical, too! The one that won last year was an eighteen-tier rosebud trifle with enormous pink wings. While the competition was being judged, it flew all around the room, scattering sugar rose petals on everyone."

"So what if the elves are good?" Jasmine said, lifting her chin determinedly. "I know the recipe for the chocolate cake my grandma makes, and it's delicious. And you can do magic, Trixi."

Trixi shook her head. "Not this kind of magic. Only the bakery elves can do cake magic. It takes years to learn. That's why everyone in the kingdom gets their cakes from Sugarsweet Bakery!"

"But can't you try, Trixi?" Jasmine said. "We're not going to just give up!"

Ellie nodded. "No way! We can't sit

back and let King Merry turn into a stink toad!"

"It couldn't hurt to try," Summer pleaded.

"Okay, let's do it," Trixi said. "And I know just the thing to get us started!" She hovered over their heads and tapped her ring. Suddenly she and the girls were each wearing a colourful apron. Trixi's was a soft blue with pictures of cupcakes and cookies embroidered on it in rainbow sparkles, Jasmine's was the colour of pink icing, Summer's looked like creamy lemon curd and Ellie's was the same shade of purple as the sugar flowers in the window box. "Much better," Trixi said as she rolled up her sleeves. "Now let's get baking!"

The girls marched through the kitchen

door with Trixi flying behind them on
her leaf. The bakery kitchen was an
enormous room with a stone floor and
eight big wooden tables all set up with
bowls, spoons and whisks. Six of the
tables had groups of elves clustered round
them. The elves were wearing chef's hats
and aprons and were all arguing fiercely
with one another and throwing things.
There were pots and pans
flying all over the
place. Jasmine
ducked as
a wooden
spoon
whizzed past
her head.

"You can
have that table

over there!" Albertin snapped at the girls, pointing to a spare table. "Go and see Greenbeard and give him the name of the cake you're making. He and I are the judges." Albertin gestured to an old elf with a small green beard who was holding a clipboard.

"Summer and I will go and put our names down," Ellie said. "Trixi, can you magic up all the ingredients Jasmine needs?"

"Of course," Trixi replied.

Ellie and Summer rushed over to Greenbeard.

"Yes?" he scowled.

"We'd like to enter the competition please," said Ellie politely.

"Name!"

"Summer, Ellie and—" Summer began.

"No, you sponge-brain!" Greenbeard interrupted. "Not *your* names. The name of your cake!"

"Oh." Ellie looked at Summer. "What shall we call it?" she asked.

"Grandma's Chocolate Cake?" Summer suggested.

The elf sneered. "*Grandma's Chocolate Cake!*" His voice rose scornfully and the other elves nearby turned and looked. "What sort of name is that? Here, these are the other cakes in the competition." He held the clipboard out.

Ellie read the names out loud: "Whoopsie-Daisy Upside-Down Cake, Firework-Fizzle Fudge Cake, Solo-Singing Sponge Cake, Dancing Cupcakes…" She and Summer looked at each other. Suddenly "Grandma's

Chocolate Cake" didn't sound anywhere near as exciting.

But before they could come up with a better name, Albertin started banging a large silver gong hanging on the wall. "Contestants!" he shouted. "Take your places. The competition is about to start!"

At the other workbenches, the elves were picking up spoons and bowls and bags of flour and sugar, getting ready to begin. "I guess it'll just have to stay as Grandma's Chocolate Cake," Ellie said as she and Summer hurried over to their table.

"I just hope Trixi can think of some good magic to go in it," Summer fretted.

"Contestants!" Albertin shouted. "Get ready…"

"Wait!" a screechy voice called.

"We haven't entered yet!"

The girls turned towards the door and saw three creatures with leathery wings, spiky hair and grey skin charging into the kitchen.

"Storm Sprites!" said Jasmine in horror. "Queen Malice must have sent them to make sure we don't get the silverspun sugar!"

"You're too late," Greenbeard told the sprites crossly.

"Oh, no we're not!" said the first sprite. He grabbed the clipboard, snatched the pen and scrawled something down on the list. "See! We're entered now."

"But…but…" Greenbeard spluttered.

"We're going to be making a Scrumptious Surprise Cake," declared the sprite.

"And we're going to win the silverspun sugar!" said one of the other sprites. "Storm Sprites are very good cooks, you know," he boasted.

"Better than stupid elves!" the third sprite sneered.

"Oi!" shouted one of the nearby elves. "Elves are much better cooks than sprites!"

The sprite grabbed a nearby bowl and plonked it on the elf's head. "That's what you think!" he cackled.

He and the other Storm Sprites ran to the last empty table and hopped up onto it. "We're going to win, and when we do we're not going to give you any silverspun sugar," one of them crowed at the girls. "King Merry is going to turn into a stink toad, and there's nothing you can do to stop it!"

Trixi turned to the girls in dismay. "Oh, no!" she cried. "Now what do we do?"

"Order!" Albertin yelled above the din. He banged the gong loudly again and the room went silent. "Now it's really time to get started!" he scowled. "Let the annual Sugarsweet Bakery cake-making contest begin!"

Sneaky Sprites!

"Who cares about those silly Storm Sprites," Jasmine said fiercely. "We have a cake to bake. Come on, girls. Let's get started!"

While the girls gathered up the ingredients for their cake, Trixi found a pile of cupcakes from the bakery to practise her cake magic on. She lined them all up on the table, then started muttering to herself and scratching her

head as she hovered over them. "Fly!"
she said finally, tapping her ring as she
pointed it at a cupcake. The cake rose
a few centimetres into
the air and then fell
to the floor with a
splat. "Oops!" She
giggled.

"Keep
trying, Trixi!"
Summer said
encouragingly
as she cracked
some eggs into
a bowl.

"You can do it!" Ellie called. She
grabbed an old-fashioned hand-whisk
and started to beat the eggs.

Jasmine picked up a pretty glass jar full

of brown powder and measured some out.

"Ooh!" Summer exclaimed, looking at the little jar. "Is that something magical?"

"I wish," Jasmine said. "It's only cocoa powder."

"We need something more special than that if we're going to win." Ellie sighed.

As Jasmine started mixing the cocoa powder into the eggs and Summer got the cake tins ready, Ellie looked round to see how everyone else was doing. At the table behind them, a group of elves was decorating a batch of cupcakes.

When the cupcakes were iced, the elves sprinkled a shining white powder over them and whispered a spell. The cupcakes immediately started to jump around, and some nearly jumped right off the table! The elves had a hard job keeping control of the cakes until one of them magicked up a large cage to shut them in.

The Storm Sprites were working hard too. Summer watched as they stirred an enormous bowl of strange-looking bright-orange cake mixture. Summer frowned as she stared at them. She was sure there had been three Storm Sprites before, but now there were only two. Where was the other one?

She scanned the room and caught sight of him creeping past the tables of cake-making elves, his eyes gleaming sneakily. "Look at that Storm Sprite," she whispered, nudging Ellie and Jasmine.

The sprite had his gaze fixed on a table right at the back of the room, where a group of elves were making the Firework-Fizzle Fudge Cake. It was a large cake in the shape of a Catherine wheel, covered with the most delicious-looking fudge icing. As the sprite approached the table, one of the elves added the cake magic. There was a golden flash and the cake started to spin round on the plate and shoot sparkles everywhere.

"What's that sprite doing?" Ellie asked curiously.

"I don't know, but I bet he's up to no good," Summer replied. She took a step forwards to warn the elves, but she was too late – the Storm Sprite jumped up and knocked a glass of water all over the elves' beautiful cake! He ducked out of sight behind the table and then scurried back to his own workbench just as the elves noticed the damage.

"Our cake!" cried one of the elves. "It's ruined! Now we're going to have to start all over again!"

"It was your fault!" said another elf, pointing at the first one. "You were nearest the glass."

"I didn't touch it!"

"Well, someone did, you clumsy doughnut-head!"

"It wasn't me!"

It was horrid to see the elves blaming each other. Summer hurried over to help clear things up. "Excuse me," she said. "It was—"

"Go away!" all the elves shouted at her, cutting her off.

"But I wanted to tell you that it was the—"

"Go away!" they all shrieked again

"I bet she's trying to copy our cake!" one of them said. They all looked at her fiercely.

Summer hastily returned to the others. "They wouldn't listen at all," she said sadly.

Ellie hugged her. "It's not their fault," she said comfortingly. "Queen Malice has made them all mean."

"Is there anything we can do to break her spell, Trixi?" Summer asked.

Trixi shook her head. "The elves will be nasty until the silverspun sugar has gone, and then there'll be none left for the counter-potion. We *have* to win the competition. And I need to figure out how to do cake magic…
fast!" She pointed her ring at another cupcake. "Flower!" she chanted. A burst of white flour came out of the cake, showering her with white dust. Trixi sighed.

There was a cackling laugh from nearby. The Storm Sprites were sniggering together, delighted at the sight of the dusty pixie.

"Horrible creatures!" Jasmine said. "They don't need a spell to make them mean."

"Don't worry, Trixi," Summer said kindly. "I'm sure you'll work it out in time."

"I hope the sprites don't try and ruin any other cakes," Ellie murmured as she watched the awful creatures. The sprites noticed her watching them and started pulling ugly faces. Then they clustered together, whispering. "I don't like it," Jasmine agreed.

"They're planning something else. I'm sure of it!"

"I know," whispered Ellie. "Let's each keep an eye on a sprite. That way we can stop them from causing any more trouble."

As Ellie spoke, one of the sprites left the others and approached the table where the Dancing Cupcakes were being decorated. "I'll follow that one!" she said in a low voice. "Whatever he's planning, I won't let him get away with it!"

Up to No Good!

Ellie followed the Storm Sprite as he wove between the tables. His eyes were locked on the cage full of jumping cupcakes, and he was giggling to himself sneakily. The three elves round the table were all busy arguing over what colour icing to use, and didn't notice as the sprite reached out towards the cage.

"No!" gasped Ellie, but it was too late. In one swift movement, the sprite flipped the catch on the cage and pulled the door open. The cupcakes all leaped out and started jumping off the workbench and down onto the floor.

The cupcake elves began yelling and darting around, trying to grab the escaping cakes.

Ellie bent down to help. She managed to grab a pink cupcake. It shook and tried to jump out of her hands as she carried it over to the cage. She held it as tightly as she could without squashing it, and managed to gently place it back into the cage before it could wriggle free.

One of the other elves from the Firework-Fizzle Fudge Cake table came over to help too. He caught three of them and spent a while putting them into the cage. Meanwhile, Ellie chased after a purple cupcake as it hopped towards the door. She caught it just in time and put it back with all the others.

As soon as all the cupcakes were back in the cage, one of the elves slammed the door shut and glared at her. "Stop spying on us!" he shouted at her. "Go back to your own table!"

"I was only trying to help," Ellie protested.

"Well *don't*!" The elf turned his back on her.

Ellie walked back over to her station.

"Ignore them," Summer told her as she

watched Jasmine take their cake out of the oven. "It's not their fault they're being so rude. I'm sure they don't mean it."

"Yeah," agreed Jasmine. "Now let's get on with making the icing and filling for our cake. Time is running out, and we still have lots to do!"

The girls took turns whisking the chocolate icing until it was smooth. While Summer was stirring, Jasmine looked up and groaned. Two of the Storm Sprites were laughing by their table, but the third had disappeared. She searched the room and spotted the missing sprite sneaking up on the table where the elves were making the Whoopsie-Daisy Upside-Down Cake. "Oh, no," she told the others. "They're up to no good again! Summer, can you keep mixing?"

Summer nodded, and Jasmine rushed after the sprite.

The Whoopsie-Daisy Upside-Down Cake was the lightest, fluffiest meringue cake Jasmine had ever seen. There was cream oozing out of the middle and tiny silver stars dotted all over it. It looked delicious!

As the sprite crept closer, the cake lifted into the air and flipped itself over three times before floating gently back down and landing on its plate. The elves who had made it clapped themselves on the back proudly.

Jasmine smiled in delight. She had never seen a cake do somersaults before!

Then she noticed the sprite. He was crouching on the floor, taking a tin of pepper out of his pocket. It looked like he was going to throw it over the cake to make it taste horrible.

"It just needs a little more sugar, I think," said one of the elves as he watched the cake do another flip.

"Here, I've got some to spare!" called an elf from the Solo-Singing Sponge Cake table, holding out a small bowl of white crystals.

The elf hurried forward to hand the bowl over, but didn't see the sprite crouched down on the ground. "Argh!" he yelled as he tripped over the sprite and they both went flying.

The pepper tin flew out of the sprite's hand and slid across the floor towards

Jasmine. She
grabbed it
quickly as the
elf and the
sprite shouted
at each other.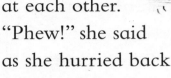
"Phew!" she said
as she hurried back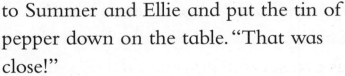
to Summer and Ellie and put the tin of
pepper down on the table. "That was
close!"

"Attention, bakers!" Albertin's voice
boomed from across the room. "You have
five minutes of cooking time left!"

"Five minutes!" gasped Ellie. "We're
never going to be ready in time!"

Jasmine looked at the two halves of
their cake, which were still cooling on
a wire rack. They'd spent so much time

trying to stop the sprites from spoiling everyone else's cakes that they hadn't even begun decorating their own yet!

"We'll have to be," Jasmine said as she started to spread melted chocolate on the top of one half of the cake. "So let's get moving!"

"Don't worry, Ellie," Summer said reassuringly. "We'll get it done somehow."

Ellie got to work spooning the thick rich chocolate filling onto the top of the other half of the cake while Summer finished mixing the icing.

"Have you been able to do any cake magic yet, Trixi?" Summer asked.

"I think I've got it!" the little pixie cried. She tapped her ring and the cupcake in front of her turned a beautiful pink colour and then transformed into a heart shape. But the cupcake didn't stop there. It got bigger and bigger…until it burst, scattering crumbs everywhere!

"Oh, no!" moaned Trixi. "I need more time!"

"I wish we could just stop the clock," said Ellie desperately.

Summer gasped. "But we can, of course!" she cried. "We can use the icy hourglass the snow brownies gave us. It can stop time, remember?"

"Brilliant!" said Jasmine. "We just need to get it from the Magic Box."

Suddenly there was a silver flash, and the Magic Box appeared on the table!

Judging Time

As Trixi and the girls watched, the lid of the Magic Box opened to reveal the six special gifts. Ellie carefully lifted the icy hourglass out of the box and held it up in front of her.

"Quick!" said Jasmine, glancing at the kitchen clock. "Turn it over! We only have ten seconds left!"

Ellie tipped the hourglass over. Instantly,

everyone apart from the girls and Trixi stopped still in the middle of whatever they were doing. Elves stood like statues as they carried their cakes towards the judges' bench. Sparkles from the firework cake were frozen in midair. The sprites were stuck too, crowded round their bright-orange cake as they finished it off with blue icing.

"Brilliant!" cried Summer. "Now we've got time to decorate our cake."

"We'd better be quick," Trixi warned, looking at the sand trickling through the hourglass. "The magic won't last for long."

The girls quickly started work. "The filling's all done," Ellie said a few moments later, finishing it off with a flourish.

"And the top is ready too," said Jasmine, putting the top half of the cake on the bottom half and using a knife to smooth the yummy melted chocolate down over the sides.

"It looks delicious!" Summer said hungrily.

"Let's try it," said Jasmine, scraping some leftover bits out of the cake tin. She dipped them in the chocolate filling and passed them out. She even found a tiny crumb for Trixi to taste.

It was the nicest chocolate cake Summer had ever eaten. The inside was light and gooey, and the chocolate icing on top was thick and creamy. "It's delicious, Jasmine!" she declared.

"Perfect!" Ellie agreed.

Jasmine looked pleased. "It tastes just like my grandma's!"

"We just need some magic now, Trixi," Ellie said.

"Um…well…" Trixi flew up and down above the cake anxiously.

"You can do it, Trixi!" Summer said encouragingly.

"But please hurry!" Jasmine said, pointing to the hourglass, which only had a few pink snowflakes left to run out. "Our time is almost up!"

Trixi tapped her ring and silver

sprinkles rained down, completely covering the cake in sparkly glitter.

"Brilliant!" said Summer. "Well done, Trixi!"

"What kind of magic is it?" Jasmine asked eagerly. "Has it worked?"

But before Trixi could reply, the last flakes of pink snow fell into the bottom of the hourglass and everyone around them unfroze. The kitchen was suddenly full of noise again.

"Last ten seconds!" Albertin shouted. "Ten, nine, eight, seven…"

"Quick!" said Ellie. "Let's get the cake up there!"

The three girls carried their cake over to the judges' table as quickly and carefully as they could. They put it down beside the others just as Albertin banged the gong that signalled the end of the competition.

Jasmine breathed a sigh of relief and then looked at the rest of the cakes. She bit her lip. All the other entries looked incredible. Even the sprites' cake looked impressive – it had three tall tiers, and on the top was a circle of spikes that looked just like Queen Malice's crown. The Whoopsie-Daisy Upside-Down Cake was rising in the air and flipping over and over again. The Firework-Fizzle Fudge Cake was spinning round and round with amazing purple and pink sparkles exploding off it. The Dancing Cupcakes, all decorated beautifully with silver flowers and stars, were skipping around their plate.

Jasmine looked at the chocolate cake that they'd made. It looked very ordinary compared to all the other cakes. She really hoped Trixi's magic was going to make it do something wonderful.

"The judges will now taste the cakes!" Albertin's voice rang out.

He and Greenbeard walked along the row of cakes. First of all they stopped by the Solo-Singing Sponge Cake, which was decorated with hundreds of multicoloured musical notes. "It should sing beautifully when it is cut," Trixi whispered to the girls. But to everyone's surprise, when Albertin cut into it, a horrible shriek echoed round the room.

The elves who had made the cake looked shocked. "It shouldn't sound like that!" one cried.

The judges covered their ears and tasted it. "It tastes nice, but sounds awful," said Albertin.

Greenbeard nodded. "Two out of ten."

The two judges moved on to the Dancing Cupcakes, but as they tasted them they each pulled a face. "They're very bitter!" said Albertin, shaking his head. "But they are nice and magical. Three out of ten for the Dancing Cupcakes!"

And so it went on. Every single cake seemed to have something wrong with it. The Firework-Fizzle Fudge Cake ran out of sparkles and drooped in the middle when it stopped spinning, and the Whoopsie-Daisy Upside-Down Cake was so salty that the judges had to drink a large glass of water after tasting it.

"This is your fault!" one of the Whoopsie-Daisy Sponge Cake elves shouted at one of the Solo-Singing

Sponge Cake elves. "You said you were giving us sugar, not salt!"

An elf from the Dancing Cupcake table pointed at one of the Firework-Fizzle Fudge Cake elves. "And you were supposed to be helping catch our cupcakes, but I bet you did something to them when you put them back in the cage. I thought you were there for a long time!"

There was sudden uproar as all the elves started accusing one another of ruining their cakes. The girls looked round in astonishment. "The elves must have been sabotaging one another's cakes without us realising," said Ellie. "We were so busy watching the Storm Sprites, we didn't realise the elves were up to no good all along!"

"Well, maybe we still have a chance," said Summer hopefully. "There's just ours and the sprites' cake left now."

The girls watched nervously as the judges turned to their cake. They cut into it and everyone sighed hungrily. It looked chocolatey and delicious. The filling was soft and dark, the melted chocolate on top was thick and sweet and the sparkles made it look extra special.

Albertin took a tiny bite, chewed, and then took another. He started to smile. Greenbeard did the same. "Mmmm," they said to each other, nodding.

"Delicious!" said Albertin, taking another mouthful.

"Really excellent!" said Greenbeard.

"What magic did you put in?" Ellie whispered to Trixi.

"I—" Trixi started to say, but Albertin interrupted her.

"A very tasty cake, but not magical at all."

The girls looked puzzled.

"I'm so sorry!" Trixi shook her head sadly. "I couldn't make the cake magic work, so I just put some silver sprinkles on top!"

"You did your best," Ellie said kindly.

"Well, if you couldn't do cake magic, maybe the sprites couldn't either!" Jasmine said hopefully.

The girls held hands as Albertin cut into the Storm Sprites' orange and blue cake. Suddenly each of the spikes on the sprites' cake let out a stream of blue icing that trickled down the tiers, making the cake look like a beautiful fountain!

"Ooh!" the elves cried.

"Aaahh!" said the judges.

"But how did the sprites get cake magic?" Ellie cried.

"They must have stolen it from the elves!" Jasmine sighed.

Summer and Trixi turned away as Albertin put his fork into the cake. They couldn't bear to look.

Jasmine and Ellie held their breath as they watched Albertin put the spoonful in his mouth...

"Eugh!" he spluttered, spitting it out.

"Revolting!"

"Truly horrible!"
agreed
Greenbeard,
spitting his
mouthful out too.
"What's in this
cake?"

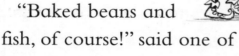

"Baked beans and
fish, of course!" said one of
the sprites in surprise.

"Mmmm, delicious!" said another,
grabbing a handful for himself. "This is
what cakes should taste like!"

Albertin and Greenbeard ducked their
heads together and whispered for a
minute, and Albertin held his hand up for
silence. "We have chosen a winner!" he
announced. "The sprites' cake gets two

out of ten for its magic fountain display.
But the only cake that we'd like to try
more of is…Grandma's Chocolate Cake!
Jasmine, Summer, Ellie and Trixi win,
with eight out of ten!"

"It may not be magical," Greenbeard
said, "but it looks wonderful and it tastes
spectacular! It's the best chocolate cake I
have *ever* eaten. We must have the recipe
for our bakery!"

The girls gasped in disbelief.

"I can't believe we won the contest!"
Jasmine cried.

"Better than that," Summer squealed,
"we've won the silverspun sugar!"

The girls held hands and jumped up
and down while Trixi looped and spun
happily above them on her leaf.

Greenbeard and Albertin opened two

huge boiled-sweet doors and suddenly the kitchen was filled with a tinkling sound, which was coming from the courtyard outside.

"The silver sugar tree!" the elves all cried as they rushed outside into the large paved courtyard. In the centre was a tree with gorgeous silver leaves that were making a noise like lots of little bells tinkling as the breeze rushed through them.

"And that must be the silverspun sugar!" cried Ellie, pointing to where stands of wispy silver floss were appearing on the branches.

"Yes." Trixi sighed. "Isn't it beautiful?"

In a few minutes, the whole silver tree was covered in the fluffy silver balls. Albertin waved his hand and all the balls

floated off the branches
and down into a large
flour bag that he was
holding.

"Here's your prize,"
he told the girls,
holding the bag out
to them. "Silverspun
sugar!"

Jasmine stepped forward to take it, but
before she could, one of the Storm Sprites
dived in front of her. "We'll have that!" he
cackled, swiping it out of Albertin's hands.

"No!" gasped Jasmine.

But it was too late. The Storm Sprite
was running away – with the precious
bag of silverspun sugar in his hands!

Stop that Sprite!

Trixi acted instantly. She tapped her ring and called out a spell:

"Icing sugar, coat the ground.
Make that sprite slip all around!"

There was a white flash and a big puddle of wet icing sugar suddenly appeared in front of the Storm Sprite.

He tried to stop, but he skidded straight into it. "Wahhhh!" he yelled, his arms flailing. The bag of silverspun sugar flew out of his grasp and high into the sky as the sprite landed on his bottom in the middle of the icing sugar.

"Oh, no!" Summer cried as the bag plummeted towards the ground.

"I'll get it!" Trixi called, zooming towards it and tapping her ring. The bag stopped in midair just before it hit the ground.

"Hooray!" called the girls.

Trixi grinned. "I'll take this straight to Maybelle so that she can put it in the potion," she told the girls. "Once it's gone, the elves should return to their usual selves." She tapped her ring a final time and called "I'll be right back!" as a purple whirlwind spun round her and the bag, whisking them away.

"Noooo!" A loud snarl ripped through the air, making the leaves of the silver sugar tree tremble.

Jasmine, Summer and Ellie watched in horror as the iron gates at the end of the courtyard flew open with a crash and Queen Malice's round black carriage swept in, pulled by the two giant enchanted rats.

"You infuriating children!" hissed Queen Malice, standing up on the driver's seat. "And you useless sprites, letting them win the silverspun sugar! I'll make you pay for this, all of you!" She pounded her staff on the ground and the rats leaped forward, pulling her along behind. "Rats — eat whatever you can find!"

Everyone gasped as the rats
raced toward the kitchen.

Jasmine turned to
the elves. "Are you
going to let Queen
Malice wreck your
bakery?" she called.

But the elves
all looked a little
bit dazed. They
didn't look as grumpy
as they had before, and they were all
rubbing their heads in confusion as if
they weren't sure why they had been so
cross.

"Queen Malice's spell is wearing
off!" Summer exclaimed. "The elves are
turning nice again!"

"We can't have rats in our kitchen!"

gasped Albertin. "They'll eat everything!"

"Not if we can help it!" Jasmine said, running in front of the bakery doors and grabbing a rolling pin and a pan from an elf as she went. She bashed the rolling pin against the pan to make a loud noise.

The rats stopped, looking startled.

"Forward!" Queen Malice yelled, pounding her staff on the ground angrily.

"It's working!" Ellie shouted to the elves. "Grab a pan!" She started clanging two metal spoons together, and the rats took a step backwards.

Just then Trixi reappeared overhead in a purple whirlwind.

"Trixi, help!" Jasmine called. "Can you get rid of the rats?"

"I'll try!" the little pixie said bravely. She tapped her ring and chanted:

"Giant rats, turn small once more.
Don't take Queen Malice through
that door!"

A stream of purple glitter flew out of Trixi's ring and surrounded the rats, who started shrinking back to their normal size. The harness dropped away from them and the carriage tipped forwards with such a jolt that Queen Malice was sent tumbling out, straight into the puddle of icing next to her Storm Sprite!

She shrieked with anger, white icing sugar dripping off her bony face and turning her black hair grey. The sprites looked shocked for a moment, and then started to snigger.

"You dare to laugh at me?" Queen Malice screamed at them, getting to her feet.

The rats looked at their mistress and then turned tail and raced away, out through the courtyard gates and into the woods beyond.

Queen Malice strode over to her carriage. "Never mind," she said, a cruel smile creeping onto her face. "You useless Storm Sprites can pull me!" She pointed her staff at the three Storm Sprites. There was a flash of green light and suddenly the sprites were attached to the front of the carriage. Queen Malice got inside and cracked her whip through the air. "Move!" she shrieked.

Flapping their leathery wings, the sprites rose into the air and flew the carriage away.

There was a moment's silence, then everyone started talking at once.

"Oh my goodness, wasn't Queen Malice angry!" said Jasmine.

"She was furious!" Summer giggled.

"And covered in icing sugar!" Ellie grinned. "Oh, Trixi. You were brilliant!"

Trixi hung her head. "I still feel bad for not being able to do cake magic," she said sadly.

"That doesn't matter," Summer said. "You might not be able to do bakery elf cake magic, but you're brilliant at pixie magic!"

"Yes, you turned the rats small and you stopped the sprite from stealing the silverspun sugar," Jasmine added. "We wouldn't have got it back if it wasn't for you."

Trixi smiled. "It was pretty funny seeing the Storm Sprite fall into that puddle of wet icing sugar," she admitted.

"And now we have the second ingredient for King Merry's counter-potion," Summer said encouragingly.

Albertin clapped his hands. "This calls for a celebration! I think we all need something to eat. Everyone help yourself to anything you want from the bakery."

"Though I'd avoid trying any of the other competition entries," added Greenbeard with a chuckle.

The girls and elves all rushed inside and feasted on the cakes and cookies, muffins and doughnuts. Ellie had a cherry slice that made her hair turn even redder than normal, Jasmine ate a piece of lemon sherbet cake that fizzed and popped in her mouth with every bite and Summer had a 'Light as a Feather' strawberry tart that flew around her head three times before she could eat it. Greenbeard handed round large glasses of iced fruit punch and everyone agreed that the girls' chocolate cake was the most delicious that they had ever tasted. The last three slices were saved for Ellie, Summer and Jasmine.

When they finished, Ellie patted her tummy. "You know, I don't think I could eat another thing!" she said with a sigh.

"Me neither," said Summer. "I'm stuffed!"

"I think that means that it's time for you to go home." Trixi smiled.

"We'll come back as soon as we can," Jasmine promised.

"I'll send you a message in the Magic Box as soon as Aunt Maybelle works out the next ingredient we need for King Merry's counter-potion," Trixi told them. She swooped around and kissed them each on the tip of their nose.

The girls held hands. "Goodbye!" they called to the elves.

"Bye!" cried the elves. "Thank you for the delicious chocolate cake!"

"We'll make it in our bakery from now on!" Albertin declared. "People will come from all over the Secret Kingdom to taste Jasmine, Summer and Ellie's sparkly chocolate cake!"

"I'll tell my grandma I made it and that some friends of mine really enjoyed it!" Jasmine laughed.

"Please send our love to King Merry," Summer asked Trixi.

"I will." Trixi smiled. She tapped her ring and immediately the girls were surrounded by a whirlwind of bright purple sparkles that whisked them back home.

Jasmine, Summer and Ellie landed back with a bump in the middle of the bushes with the Magic Box safely between them.

Summer blinked. "Oh, wow. I forgot we were out here in the park."

"That was such a *yummy* trip to the Secret Kingdom!" said Jasmine, brushing away a cake crumb from her cheek.

"Our most delicious adventure yet!" Ellie grinned.

Just then they heard the sound of voices
close by, and then Finn poked his head
into the undergrowth. "Found you!" he
yelled.

The girls grinned and scrambled out of
their hiding place.

"Well done, boys!" said Summer as Finn
and his friends crowded round them.

"Finn, Summer!" Mrs Hammond called from the picnic rug. "It's time for the party tea. Who wants some cake?"

"Me, me, ME!" yelled Finn and his friends as they charged over to the picnic site.

Summer, Ellie and Jasmine looked at one another and groaned.

"I can't possibly have any more cake!" Ellie said with a laugh.

"Me neither," agreed Summer.

Jasmine grinned. "How about some more adventures, though?"

"Oh, yes!" Summer and Ellie exclaimed together.

In the next Secret Kingdom
adventure, Ellie, Summer and
Jasmine visit

Dream Dale

Read on for a sneak peek...

Bedtime's Boring!

Ellie Macdonald was playing catch
in her back garden with her two best
friends, Summer Hammond and Jasmine
Smith. Jasmine had just thrown the ball
high into the air and Ellie and Summer
were both running to catch it when
Ellie's mum opened the back door.
"Girls!" she called.

Ellie turned to look, and Summer
crashed into her with a bump. "Oops!"

she giggled as she and Ellie fell in a heap on the floor. "Sorry, are you okay?"

Ellie grinned. "I'm all right. I fall over so often anyway that I'm used to it!"

Mrs Macdonald smiled. "Whoops, sorry, girls! I just wanted to ask Ellie if she'd put Molly to bed for me. I've got a load of paperwork to catch up on this evening."

"Sure, Mum!" Ellie said. Molly was her four-year-old sister. Ellie loved being a big sister, even though Molly was a bit naughty at times!

"We'll help," offered Summer.

Mrs Macdonald smiled. "Thanks! There's some popcorn in the kitchen for all of you when you've finished." She disappeared back into the house.

"Yum!" declared Jasmine. "It won't take

us long to get Molly into bed and then we can eat the popcorn and watch a DVD."

Ellie and Summer grinned at each other.

"What?" said Jasmine, seeing their expressions. "It can't be *that* hard to put Molly to bed."

"You don't know what little brothers and sisters are like!" Ellie told her.

"Finn and Connor never go to bed without a fight!" Summer agreed, thinking of her two younger brothers.

"It'll be fine," Jasmine said airily. "After all, if we can beat Queen Malice, I reckon we can do anything!"

The girls grinned at each other. They shared an amazing secret – they could go to a magical world that no one else knew about! The Secret Kingdom was an enchanted place full of incredible creatures like mermaids, unicorns, elves and fairies. But the beautiful land was in great trouble. When lovely King Merry had been chosen to rule instead of his sister, evil Queen Malice, the wicked queen had sworn that she'd make everyone in the kingdom as miserable as she was. Summer, Ellie and Jasmine had managed to stop a lot of her terrible plans, but now she'd put a horrible curse on her own brother!

She'd given King Merry a poisoned cake that was slowly turning him into a horrible creature called a stink toad. The only way to cure the king was for him to drink a counter-potion, but to make it the girls had to find six very rare ingredients. They had to get them all and cure the king before the Summer Ball or King Merry would be a stink toad forever! The girls, Trixi and her aunt Maybelle were the only ones that knew it was happening because the pixies had cast a forgetting spell, so everyone else – including the king himself – forgot about the terrible curse. The girls had promised to do anything they could to secretly help their friend.

"At least we've found two of the ingredients for the counter-potion already," Jasmine said as they went inside to find Molly. "And hopefully we'll be called back to the Secret Kingdom to find another one soon!"

Molly was already in her pyjamas. She looked just like a younger version of

Ellie with her dark red curls and dancing green eyes. She had put all the sofa cushions on the floor and was leaping off the sofa onto them. "Hello!" she said, springing up excitedly. "Have you come to play with me?"

"No, we're not going to play with you, you little monkey," said Ellie. "It's bedtime."

"But bedtime's boring! I'll go to bed if you play shops with me first!" Molly bargained. "Pleeeease!" she added, taking Jasmine's hand and looking up at her, her green eyes wide.

"Oh, all right." Jasmine smiled at her. "Just one game."

"Mistake," Ellie whispered to Summer. Summer giggled.

"You absolutely promise you'll go to

bed after one game?" Ellie asked.

"Oh yes," answered Molly, nodding. "I promise."

It was the longest game ever. Jasmine was lining Molly's teddy bears up for what felt like the hundredth time when Ellie interrupted. "Okay, Molly, it really is bedtime now," she said firmly. "Remember, you promised."

Molly grinned at her. "I promised to go to bed – I didn't promise to go to sleep! Race you upstairs!"

She scampered away.

Jasmine groaned. "Okay, you two were right! This *is* going to go on forever!"

They went upstairs. Molly was jumping on her bed, singing loudly.

"Come on, Molly, into bed now," said Summer, going to the window and drawing the curtains.

"Don't shut them all the way!" Molly protested. "I like looking at the stars. They stop me feeling scared of the dark."

Summer left the curtains open a bit.

"I need another blanket!" Molly whined to her sister.

"Oh, all right!" Ellie sighed. She headed to her room and grabbed her blanket off her bed.

Read

Dream Dale

to find out what happens next!

Enjoy six sparkling adventures.
Collect them all!

Out now!

Secret Kingdom

A magical world of friendship and fun!

Join best friends
Ellie, Summer and Jasmine at
www.secretkingdombooks.com
and enjoy games, sneak peeks
and lots more!

You'll find great activities, competitions, stories
and games, plus a special newsletter for
Secret Kingdom friends!

Secret Kingdom Codebreaker

Sssh! Can you keep a secret? Ellie, Summer and Jasmine have written a new special message just for you! They have written one secret word of their special message in each of the six Secret Kingdom books in series two. To discover the secret word, hold a small mirror to this page and see your word magically appear!

The second secret word is: _____

When you have cracked the code and found all six secret words,
work out the special message and go online to enter the competition at

www.secretkingdombooks.com

We will put all of the correct entries into a draw and select one winner to receive a special Secret Kingdom goody bag featuring lots of sparkly gifts, including a glittery t-shirt!

You can also send your entry on a postcard to:

Secret Kingdom Competition, Orchard Books, 338 Euston Road, London, NW1 3BH

Don't forget to include your name and address.

Good luck!

Closing Date: 31st July 2013.

Competition only open to UK and Republic of Ireland residents. No purchase required. For full terms and conditions please see www.secretkingdombooks.com.

Collect the tokens from each Secret Kingdom book to get special Secret Kingdom gifts!

In every Secret Kingdom book there are three Friendship Tokens, that you can exchange for special gifts! Send your friendship tokens in to us as soon as you get them or save them up to get an even more special gift!

3 tokens
Secret Kingdom poster and collectable glittery bookmark

6 tokens
Scrummy scented stickers

8 tokens
Secret Kingdom pen

15 tokens
Glittery t-shirt

18 tokens
Secret Kingdom pink cap

To take part in this offer, please send us a letter telling us why you like Secret Kingdom. Don't forget to:
1) Tell us which gift you would like to exchange your tokens for
2) Include the correct number of Friendship Tokens for each gift you are requesting
3) Include your name and address
4) Include the signature of a parent or guardian

Secret Kingdom Friendship Token Offer
Orchard Books Marketing Department
338 Euston Road, London, NW1 3BH

Closing date: 31st May 2013

Terms and Conditions

(1) Open to UK and Republic of Ireland residents only (2) Purchase of the Secret Kingdom books is necessary (3) Please get the signature of your parent/guardian to enter this offer (4) The correct number of tokens must be included for the offer to be redeemed (5) Photocopied tokens will not be accepted (6) Prizes are distributed on a first come, first served basis whilst stocks last (7) No part of the offer is exchangeable for cash or any other offer (8) Please allow 28 days for delivery (9) We will use your data only for the purpose of fulfilling this offer (10) Prizes may vary from pictures shown. We reserve the right to offer prizes of an alternative or greater value.

www.secretkingdombooks.com

1 Friendship Token
www.secretkingdombooks.com

1 Friendship Token
www.secretkingdombooks.com

1 Friendship Token
www.secretkingdombooks.com

Secret Kingdom

Look out for the next sparkling
summer special!

Available
June 2013